# FANTASTIC BEASTS

### AND WHERE TO FIND THEM™

## MAGICAL CHARACTERS & PLACES
# COLORING BOOK

HarperCollins books may be purchased for educational, business, or sales promotional use. For information please email the Special Markets Department at SPsales@harpercollins.com.

Published in 2016 by
Harper Design
*An Imprint of* HarperCollins*Publishers*
195 Broadway
New York, NY 10007
Tel: (212) 207-7000
Fax: (855) 746-6023
harperdesign@harpercollins.com
www.hc.com

Distributed throughout North America by
HarperCollins Publishers
195 Broadway
New York, NY 10007

First published in Great Britain by HarperCollins*Publishers* 2016

Illustrations by Nicolette Caven (3, 9–11, 16–17, 19, 20, 22–8, 32–3, 36–9, 42–4, 46–51, 53–5, 60–1, 63–7, 70–2 & 76–9) & Micaela Alcaino (12, 14–15, 21, 31, 45, 52, 56–7, 69, 74 & 80)

Project Editor: Chris Smith
Design Manager: Terence Caven
Cover Design: Simeon Greenaway
Production Manager: Kathy Turtle

HarperCollins would like to thank Victoria Selover, Elaine Piechowski, Melanie Swartz & Jill Benscoter.

ISBN 978-0-06-257135-9

First printing, 2016

Printed and bound in USA

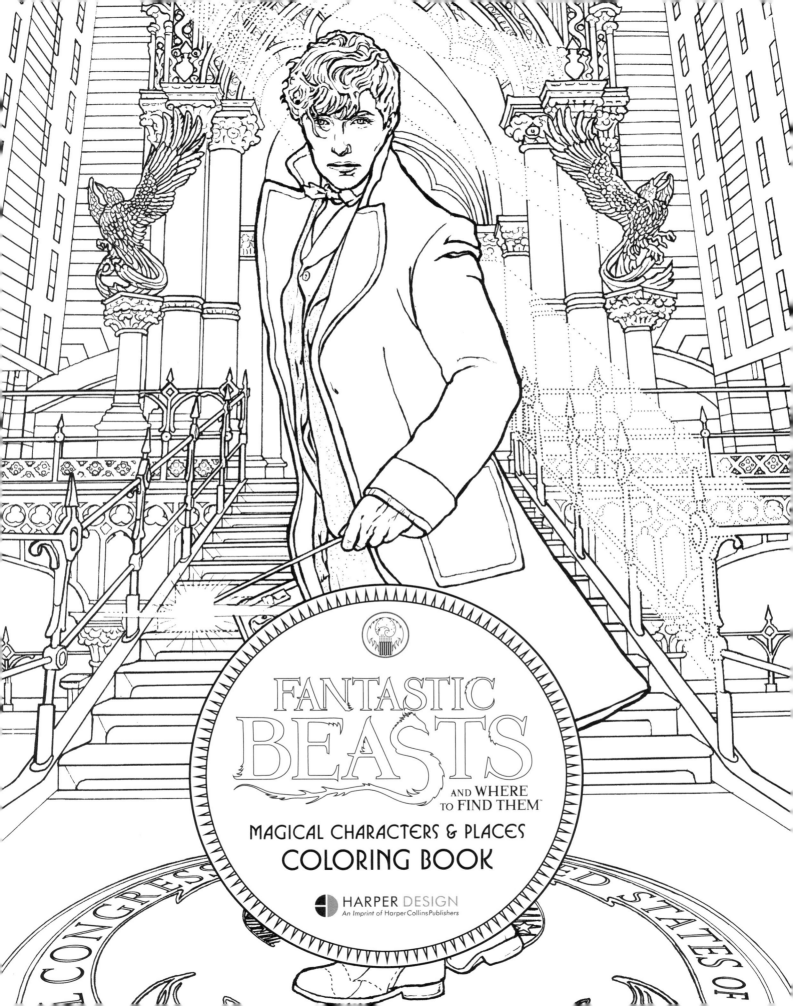

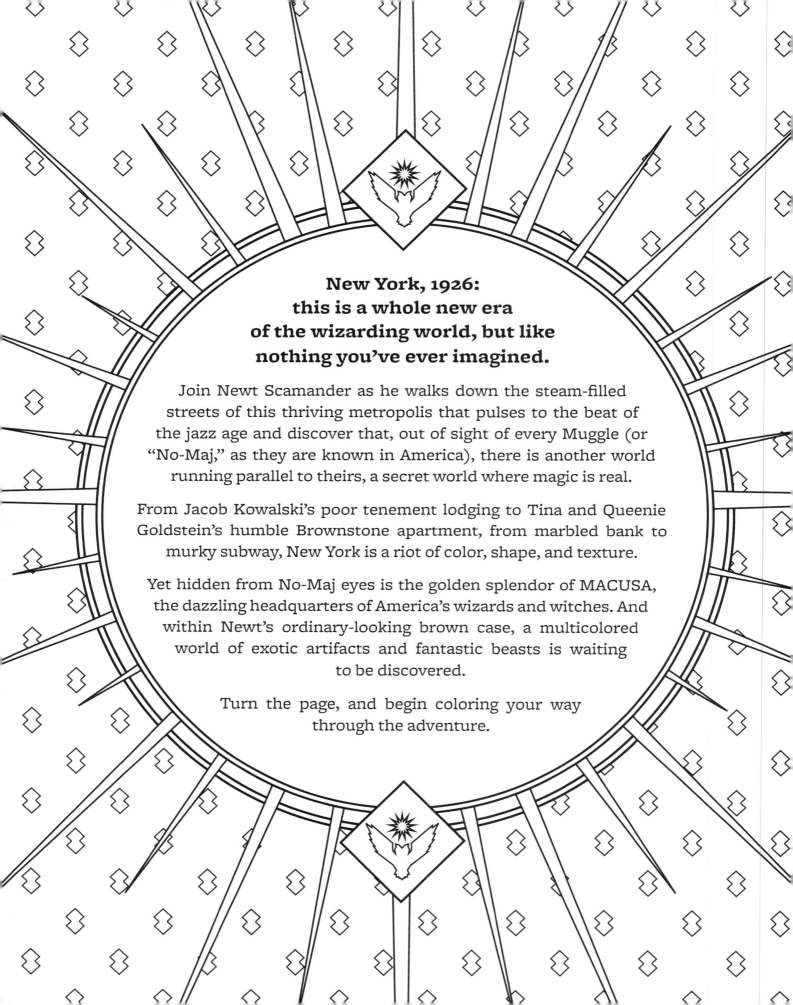

**New York, 1926:**
**this is a whole new era**
**of the wizarding world, but like**
**nothing you've ever imagined.**

Join Newt Scamander as he walks down the steam-filled streets of this thriving metropolis that pulses to the beat of the jazz age and discover that, out of sight of every Muggle (or "No-Maj," as they are known in America), there is another world running parallel to theirs, a secret world where magic is real.

From Jacob Kowalski's poor tenement lodging to Tina and Queenie Goldstein's humble Brownstone apartment, from marbled bank to murky subway, New York is a riot of color, shape, and texture.

Yet hidden from No-Maj eyes is the golden splendor of MACUSA, the dazzling headquarters of America's wizards and witches. And within Newt's ordinary-looking brown case, a multicolored world of exotic artifacts and fantastic beasts is waiting to be discovered.

Turn the page, and begin coloring your way through the adventure.

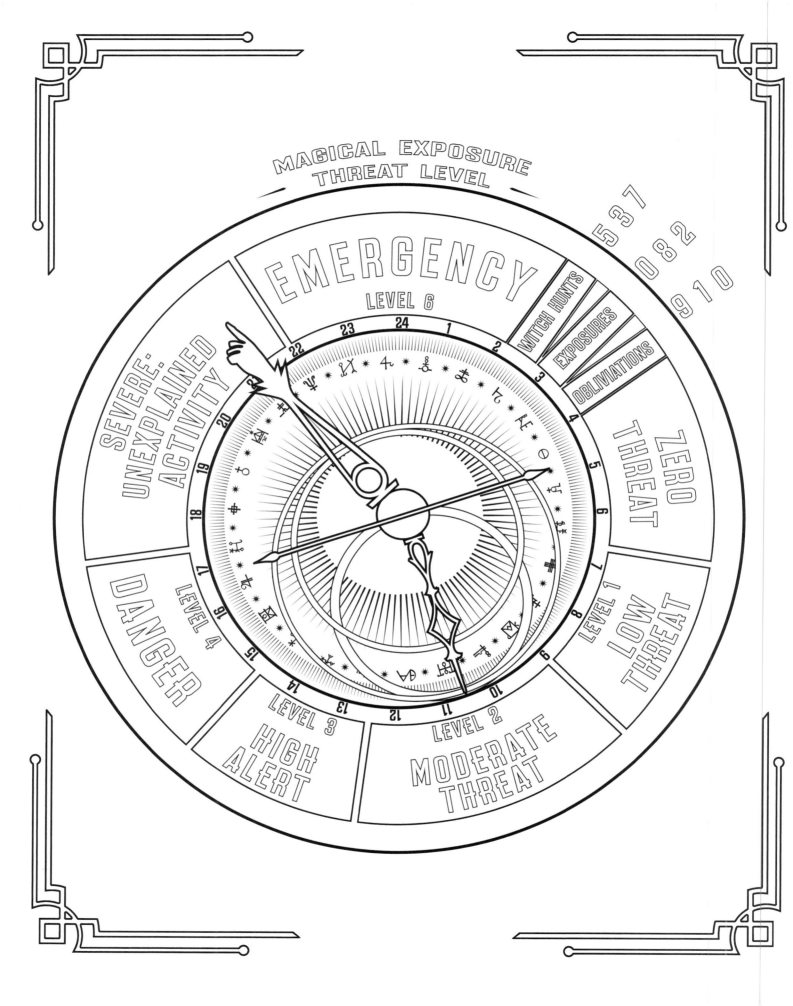

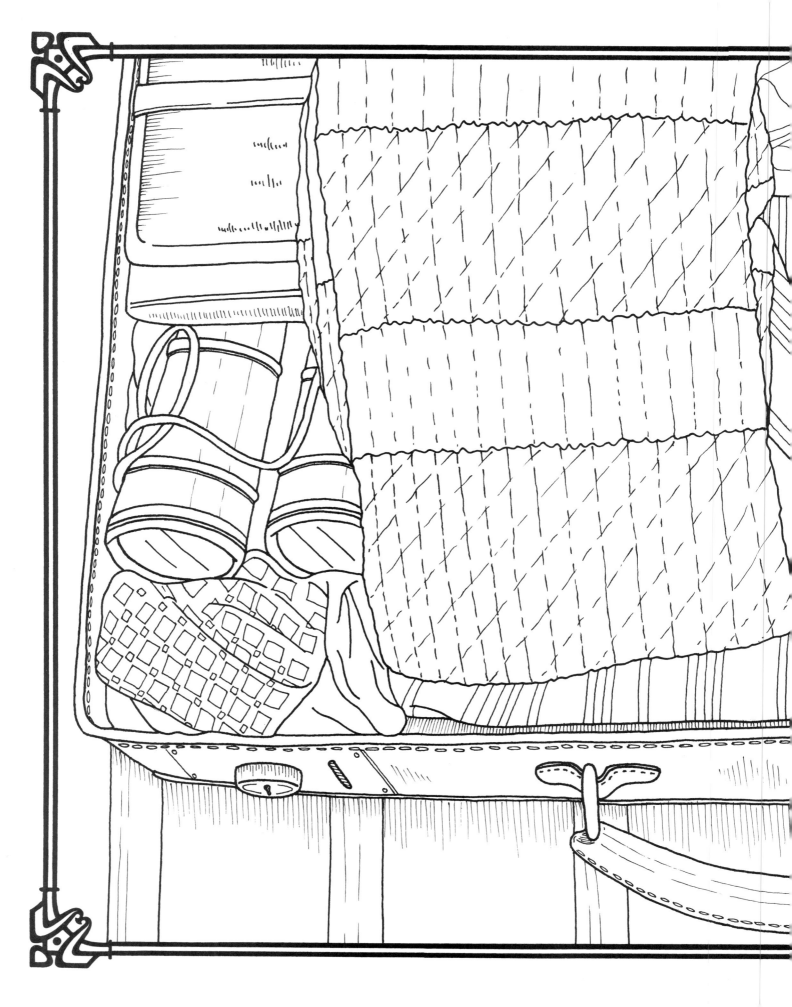

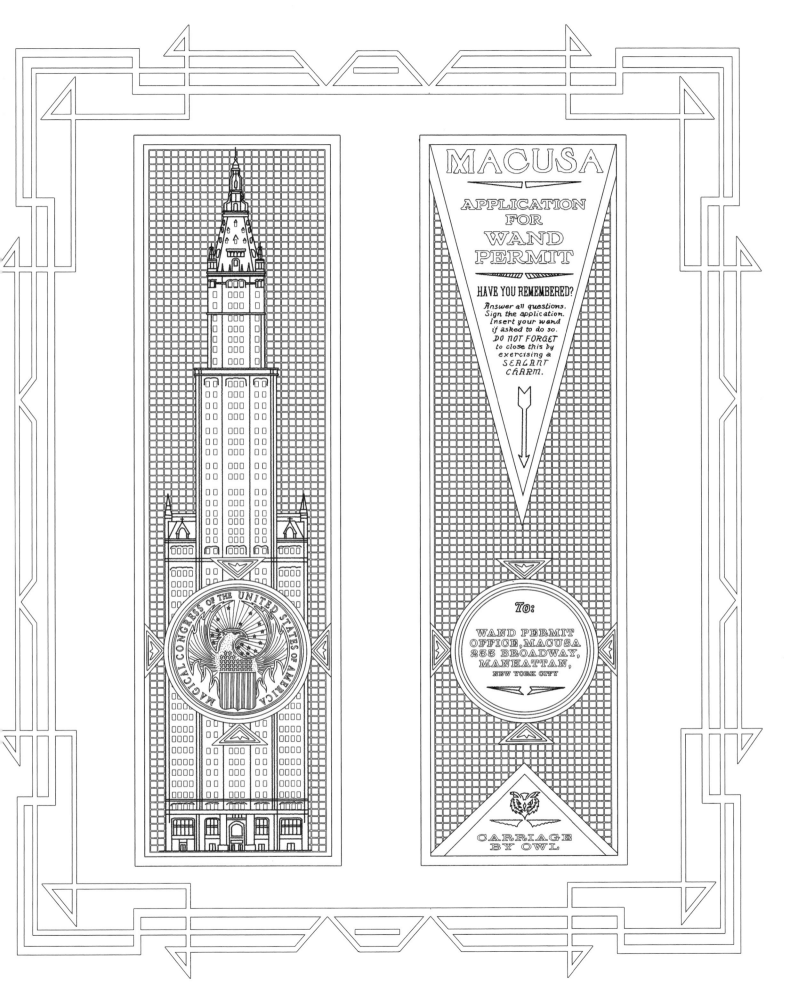

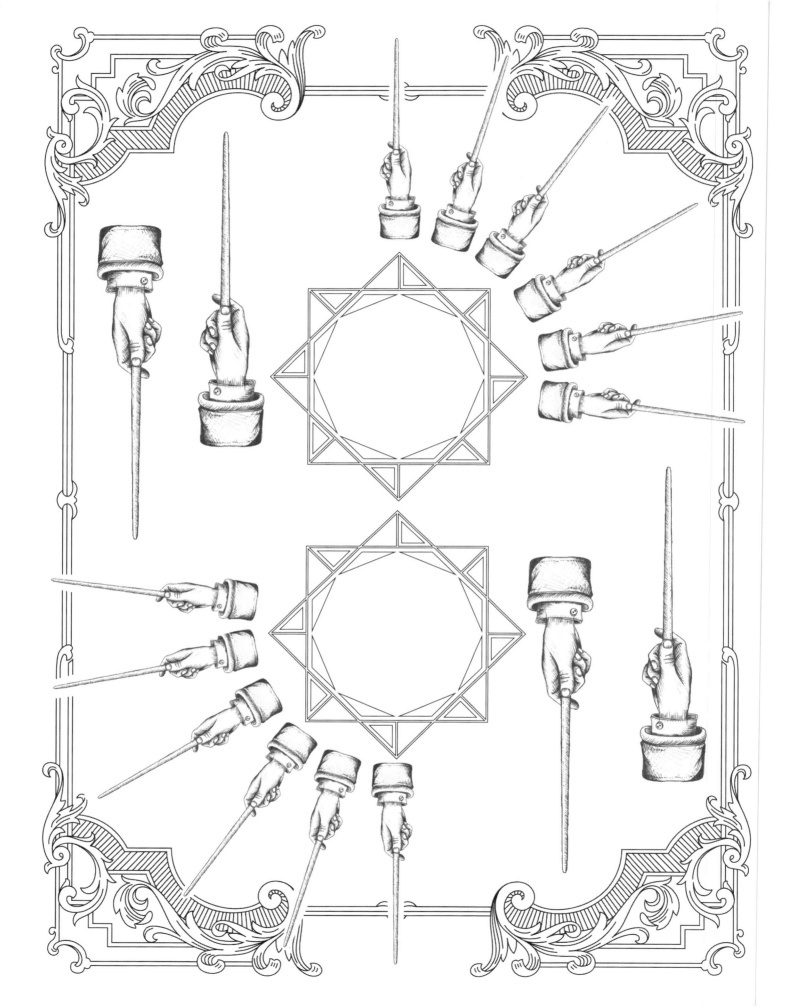

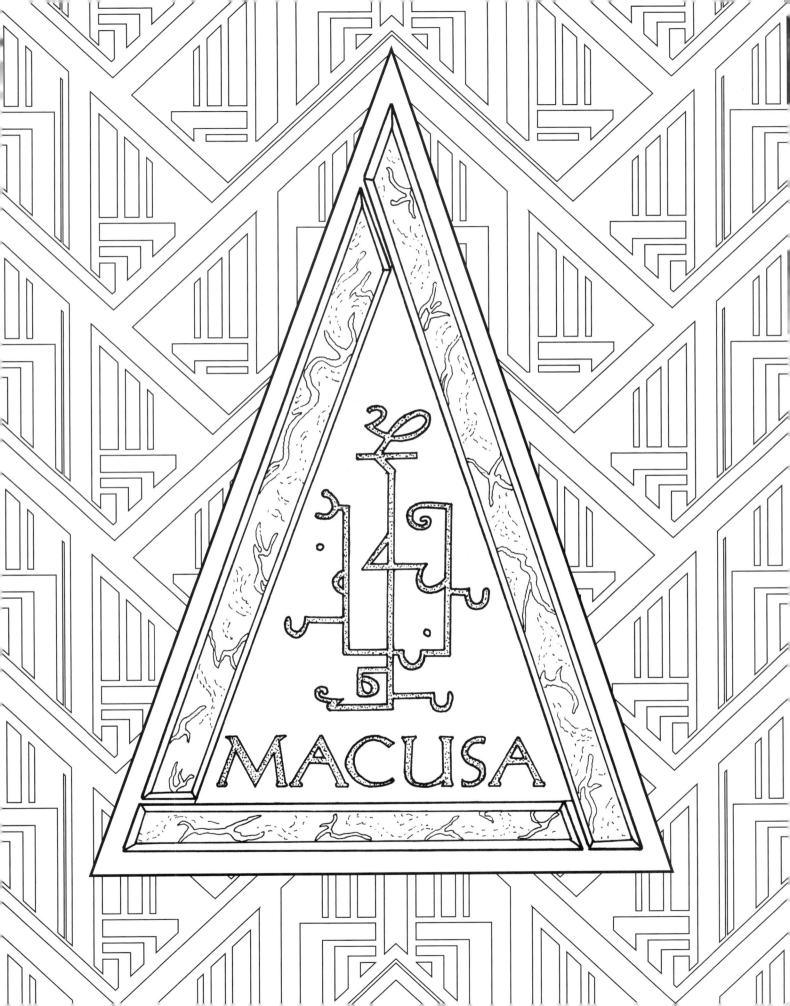

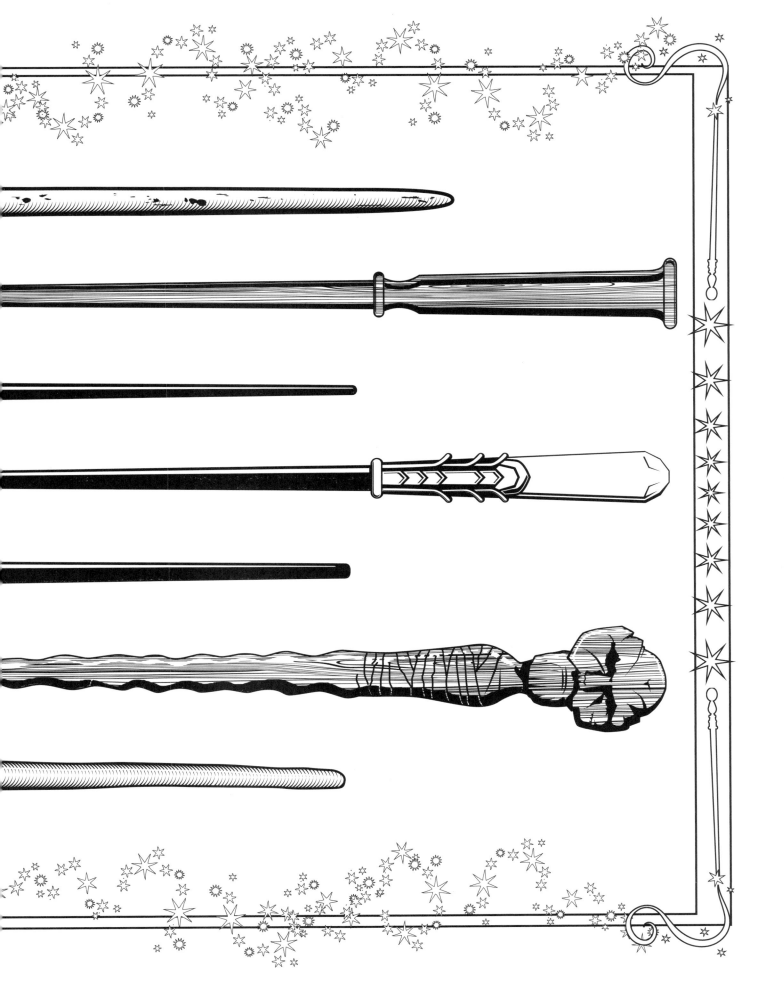

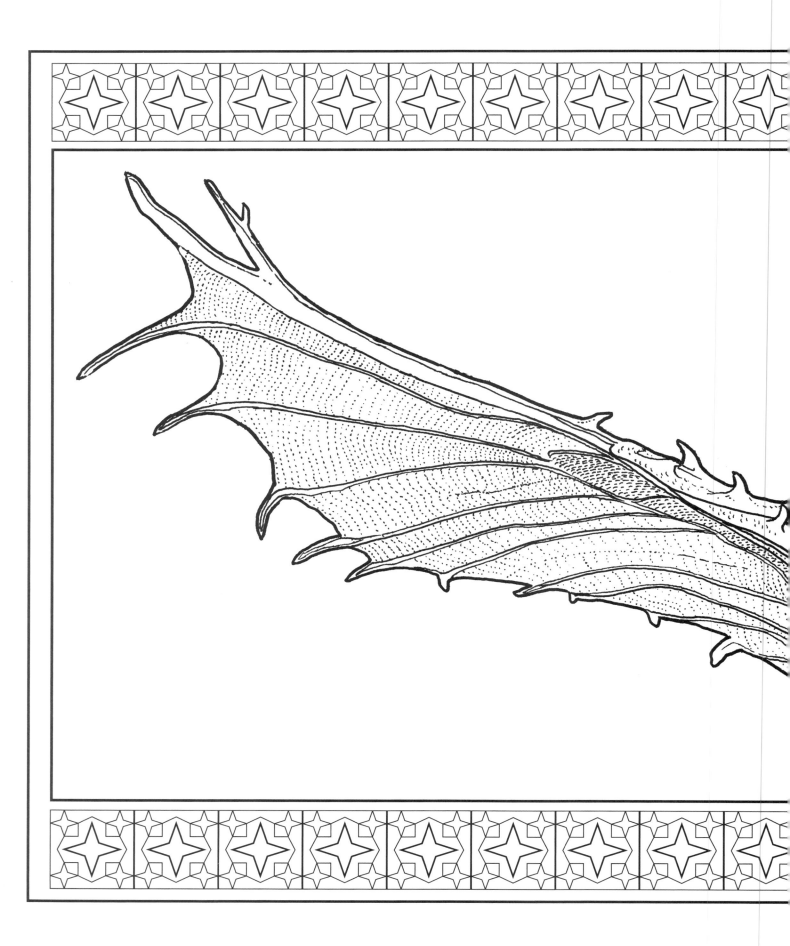

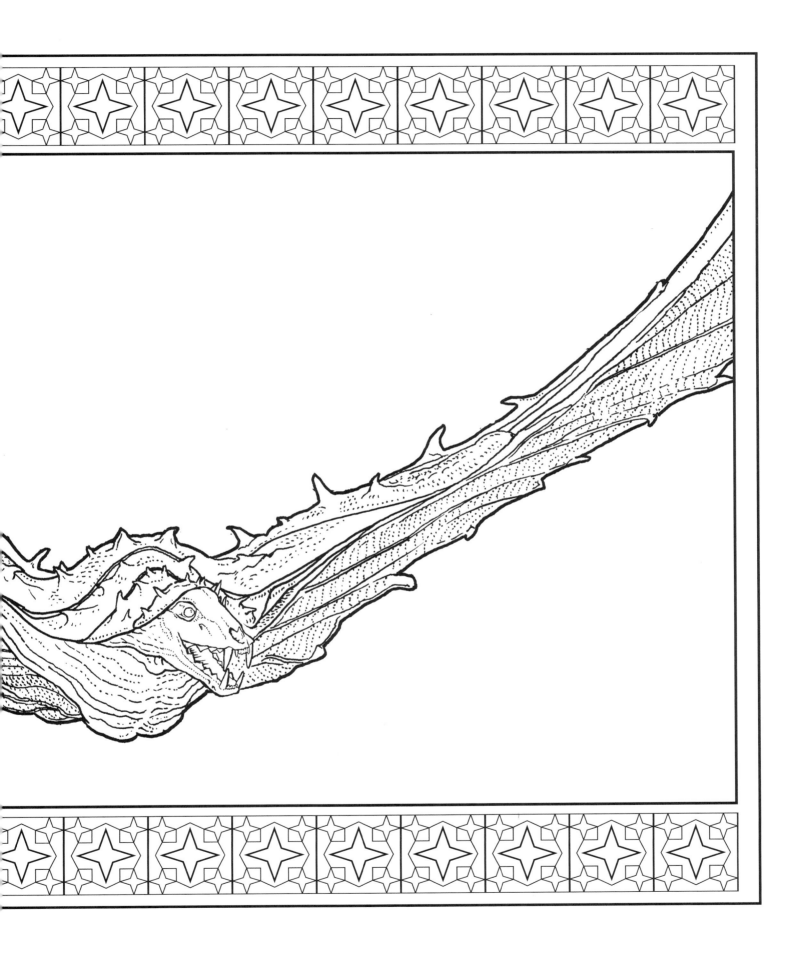

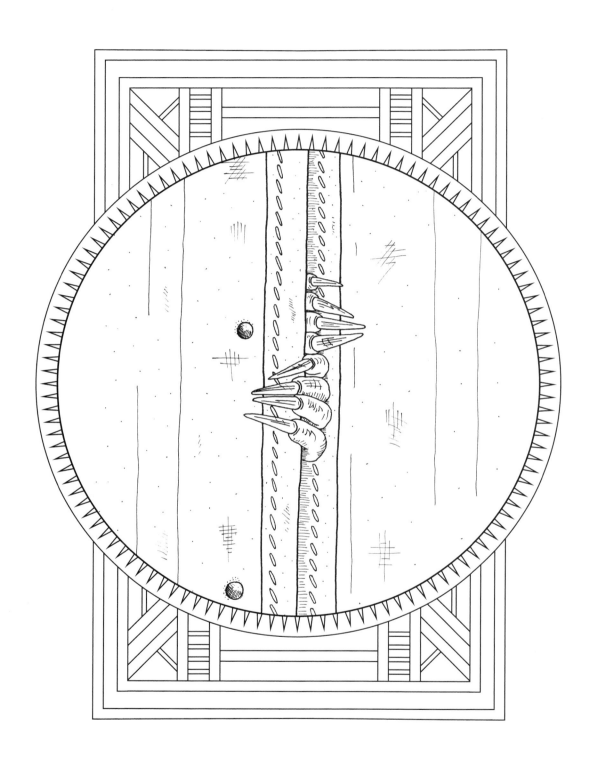